3

Here I am
with my friend.
She is Abby.

She is big
and I am bigger.
We like to sit on chairs.

Danny and Abby Are Friends

written and photographed
by
Mia Coulton

I am Danny

and I have a friend.

2

We like to eat together.

Abby eats fast

and I eat faster.

I play games

with my friend Abby.

She runs away,

and I run after her.

We play dress-up

in the closet.

She looks funny

and I look funny too.

On my walk,

I run to Abby's house.

I am at the door.

Abby runs to see me.

She is happy to see me.

I am happy

to see her too.

It is fun having a friend.